peg + cat
The Penguin Problem

JENNIFER OXLEY
+ BILLY ARONSON

WALKER
ENTERTAINMENT

One day, Peg and Cat were visiting
the very cool, very cold South Pole.
They had come to make snowmen
and to watch the Animal Winter Games.

Suddenly, four Penguins came
skiing down the hill.

3+1=4

"Sorry!" "Oops!" "My bad!"
said three of the Penguins.

"Please accept our humble apologies!"
said the fourth.

"Snow problem," said Cat,
cracking himself up.
"Get it? Like
'It's no problem'? Ha, ha!"

7+1=8

"Are you here to compete in the
Animal Winter Games?" asked Peg.

"Most certainly, yes," said a Penguin.
"But, alas, we seem to keep crashing into things."

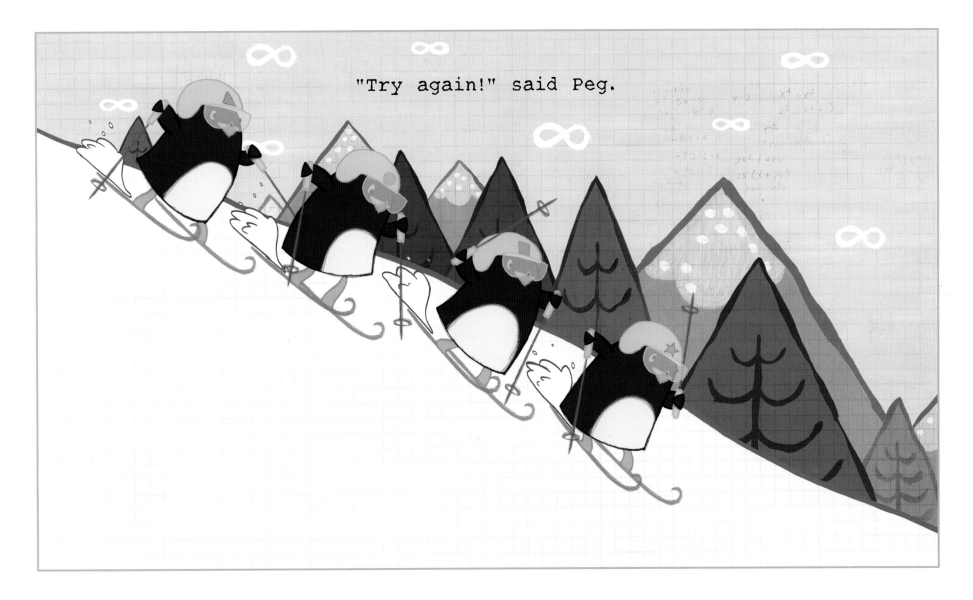

"Try again!" said Peg.

"OK!" shouted the Penguins.
"One, two, three, four!
We're the Penguins -
watch us soar!"

With that, they skied off super fast.

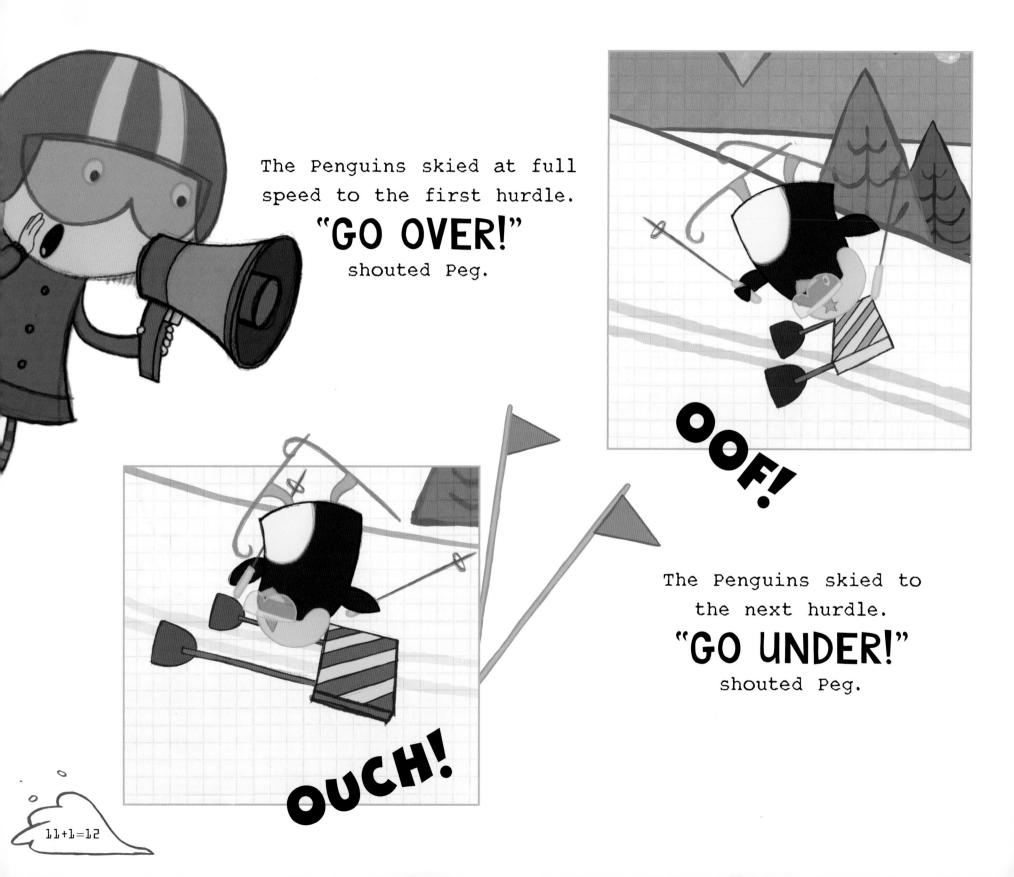

The Penguins skied at full speed to the first hurdle. **"GO OVER!"** shouted Peg.

OOF!

OUCH!

The Penguins skied to the next hurdle. **"GO UNDER!"** shouted Peg.

11+1=12

The Penguins skied
towards the flags.

"GO IN BETWEEN!"

shouted Peg.

OOF!

OUCH!

"What happened?" asked Peg.

"Well," said a Penguin,
"as it turns out, we don't know what

over, under and **in between** mean."

The other Penguins nodded.
"Not a clue," said one.

"You'll never win the race if
you don't know **over, under** and
in between!" said Peg.

"We've got a BIG PROBLEM!"

12+1=13

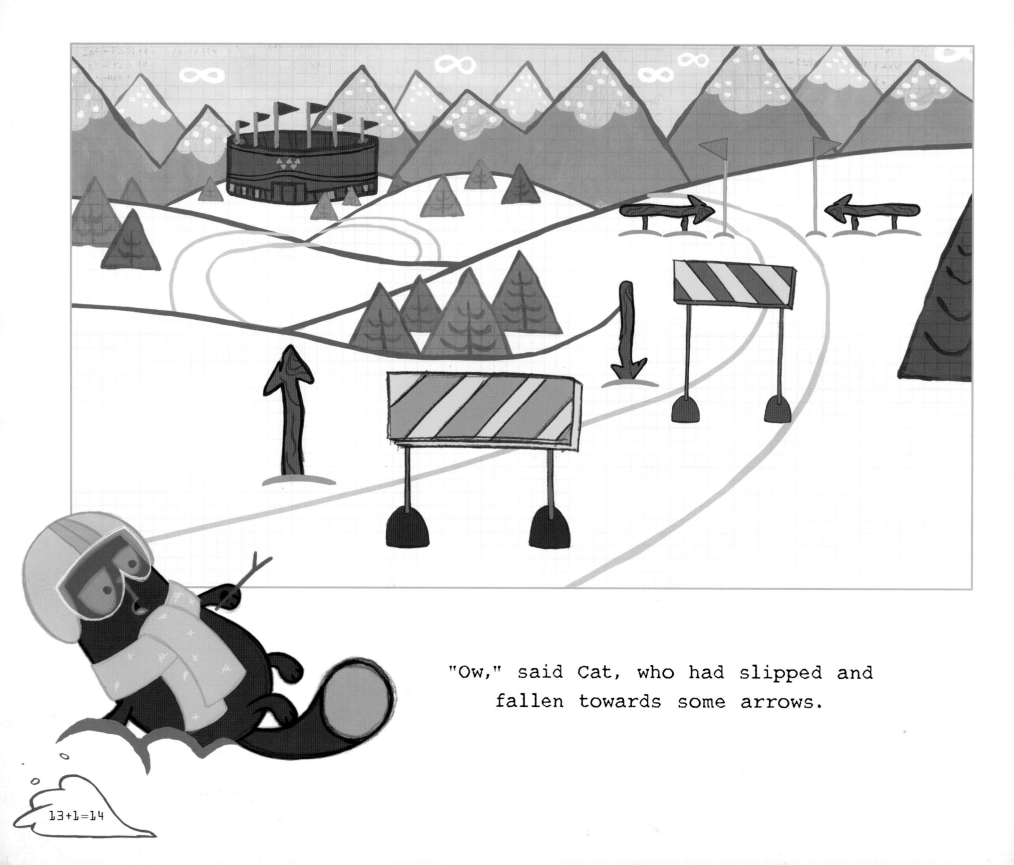

"Ow," said Cat, who had slipped and fallen towards some arrows.

The Penguins zoomed down
the hill again, this time
following the arrows.

"**Over!**" shouted Peg.
The Penguins jumped over.

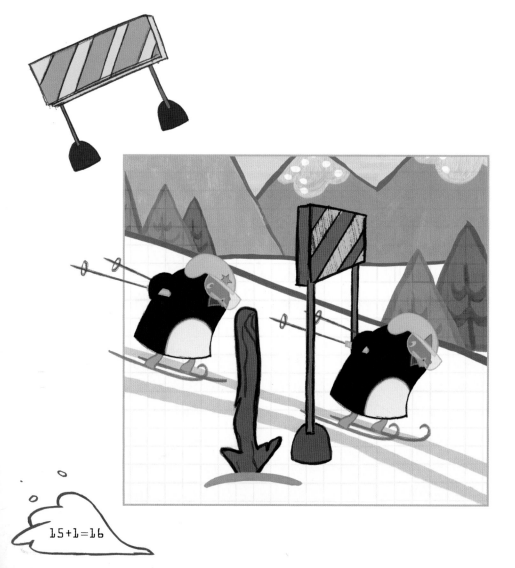

"**Under!**" shouted Peg.
The Penguins ducked under.

15+1=16

"In between!"
shouted Peg.
The Penguins skied right
in between the flags.

"They did it!"
yelled Peg.
"PROBLEM SOLVED."

16+1=17

But the problem wasn't solved.
The Penguins were skiing out of control at full speed -
away from the stadium.

"WE'VE GOT A REALLY BIG PROBLEM,"
said Peg. Peg and Cat skied along, shouting:

"Over!"

"Under!"

19+1=20

"In between!"

The Penguins skied on and on, up and down the snowy slopes,
over, under and in between things to keep from crashing.
They smashed through snow piles,
zoomed up a snow ramp and high into the air,
and did amazing midair flips
before soaring down to...

"LAND!" said a Penguin.

21+1=22

"We're not actually on land," said another Penguin.
"We seem to be on a piece of ice
in the middle of the water."

Peg heard Ramone's voice coming from the stadium.
He was announcing the start of the race-
but the Penguins couldn't reach land.

"The Penguins are missing the race!" cried Peg.
"I AM TOTALLY FREAKING OUT!"

Cat held up his paws.

22+1=23

As Peg counted, Cat dropped a big snowball...
and rolled it across Peg's ski.

"You amazing Assistant Coach Cat!" said Peg.
"If we use the skis to make a bridge,
the Penguins can go across them!"

25+1=26

In no time, the Penguins were on land and off to the races.

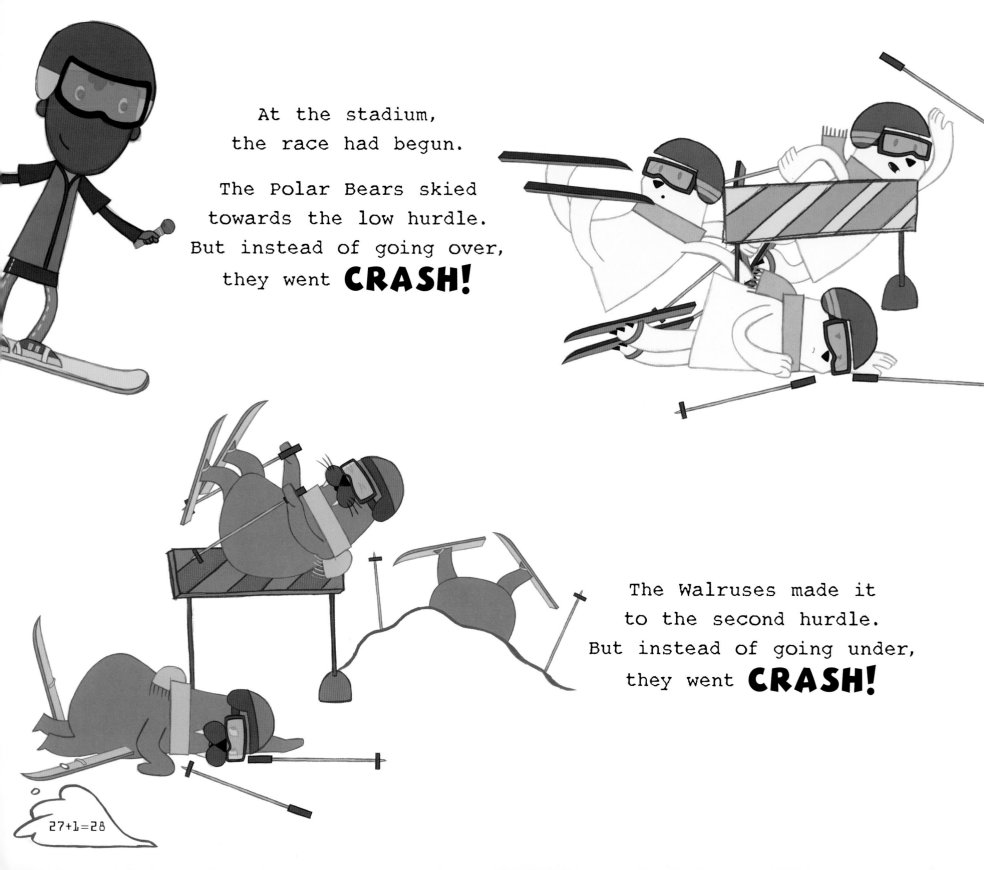

At the stadium,
the race had begun.

The Polar Bears skied
towards the low hurdle.
But instead of going over,
they went **CRASH!**

The Walruses made it
to the second hurdle.
But instead of going under,
they went **CRASH!**

27+1=28

The Squirrels made it to the flags.
But instead of going between,
they went **CRASH!**

Then the Penguins skied up to the
starting gate.

**"ONE, TWO, THREE, FOUR!
WE'RE THE PENGUINS-
WATCH US SOAR!"**
they chanted.

28+1=29

And soar they did.
The four Penguins skied

OVER

one hurdle,

UNDER

another,

29+1=30

IN BETWEEN

the flags

and all the way to

the finish line!

They were Animal Games champions!

"WOO-HOO!"

yelled their very proud coaches, Peg and Cat.

"PROBLEM SOLVED!"

30+1=31

This book is based on the TV series *Peg + Cat*.
Peg + Cat is produced by The Fred Rogers Company.
Created by Jennifer Oxley and Billy Aronson.
The Penguin Problem is based on a television script by Qui Nguyen
and background art by Erica Kepler.

First published 2016 by Walker Entertainment,
an imprint of Walker Books Ltd
87 Vauxhall Walk, London SE11 5HJ

2 4 6 8 10 9 7 5 3 1

Printed in Humen, Dongguan, China

FSC
MIX
Paper from
responsible sources
www.fsc.org
FSC® C101537

This book was typeset in OPTITypewriter.
The illustrations were created digitally.

British Library Cataloguing
in Publication Data:
a catalogue record for this book
is available from the British Library

ISBN 978-1-4063-7049-2
www.walker.co.uk